Dear Parent:
Your child's love of reading starts here!

Every child learns to read in a different way and at his or her own speed. You can help your young reader improve and become more confident by encouraging his or her own interests and abilities. You can also guide your child's spiritual development by reading stories with biblical values and Bible stories, like I Can Read! books published by Zonderkidz. From books your child reads with you to the first books he or she reads alone, there are I Can Read! books for every stage of reading:

 SHARED READING
Basic language, word repetition, and whimsical illustrations, ideal for sharing with your emergent reader.

 BEGINNING READING
Short sentences, familiar words, and simple concepts for children eager to read on their own.

 READING WITH HELP
Engaging stories, longer sentences, and language play for developing readers.

 READING ALONE
Complex plots, challenging vocabulary, and high-interest topics for the independent reader.

 ADVANCED READING
Short paragraphs, chapters, and exciting themes for the perfect bridge to chapter books.

I Can Read! books have introduced children to the joy of reading since 1957. Featuring award-winning authors and illustrators and a fabulous cast of beloved characters, I Can Read! books set the standard for beginning readers.

A lifetime of discovery begins with the magical words "I Can Read!"

Visit www.icanread.com for information on enriching your child's reading experience.
Visit www.zonderkidz.com for more Zonderkidz I Can Read! titles.

Let us love one another,
because love comes from God.
—*1 John 4:7*

The children's group
of Zondervan

www.zonderkidz.com

Sister for Sale
ISBN-10: 0-310-71469-9
ISBN-13: 978-0-310-71469-9
Copyright © 2002, 2007 by Michelle Medlock Adams
Illustrations copyright © 2002 by Karen Stormer Brooks

Requests for information should be addressed to:
Zonderkidz, Grand Rapids, Michigan 49530

Library of Congress Cataloging-in-Publication Data

applied for

Art Direction: Jody Langley
Cover Design: Sarah Molegraaf

Printed in China

07 08 09 10 • 10 9 8 7 6 5 4 3 2 1

zonderkidz

I Can Read!

BEGINNING READING 1

story by Michelle Medlock Adams
pictures by Karen Stormer Brooks

Dear God,

I need your help today.

My sister drives me mad.

How do you spell

"Sister for Sale"?

I want to write an ad.

My sister is too much for me.

She never stops all day.

She plays with music,

dolls, and paints.

She yells for me to play.

"Sister for Sale"

my ad will say—

a perfect deal for you!

She's worth about 100 bucks,

but I'll sell her for just two.

Her name is Ally Grace.

She is a little mean.

She's not the worst.

She's not the best.

She's somewhere in between.

She has blonde hair.

She has blue eyes.

She has a pointy nose.

One time she cut

her own hair short!

But that is fine.

It grows.

She blames me

when she drops her toys.

She says I made her fall.

But that's a lie.

She made it up.

That is not the truth at all.

Ally doesn't share her toys.

And she wants to play with mine.

But if you buy my sister,

she will share with you

just fine.

I need to tell you something else.

She snores a lot at night.

And if she doesn't get her way,

she may just take a bite.

But hey!

No one is perfect.

She may be nice to you.

I can sell her for one buck
in case you can't give two.

Ally Grace is funny.

She rides her bike with me.

I would keep her if I could.

But she has to go, you see.

But who will I play with?

There won't be much to do.

If you love her, God,

I guess I'll love her too.

I guess she isn't all that bad.

Sometimes she's kind of fun.

I'll keep my sister after all.

She is my only one.